Isla & Pickle

Best Friends

Kate McLelland

Picture Kelpies

D1214740

Pickle lived next door to Isla in Farmer Jess's field.
He was handsome, he was clever and he was funny.
Isla thought he was the best miniature Shetland pony
in the world!

Isla often visited Pickle in his stable and groomed his long mane. She always took him tasty snacks.

Pickle was very good at jumping over fences, so he often came to visit Isla too.

He sometimes left behind little surprises.

One day, Isla's dad asked if she would like a pet.
   "Oh, please can I have Pickle... please, Dad?" said Isla.
   "Hmm," said Dad, "I was thinking of something
a bit smaller. A rabbit, a guinea pig or maybe a goldfish?"

£32

£35

£35

£200

20% OFF
PET FOOD

FREE
FISH FOOD
(WITH EVERY
FISH)

"But I really love Pickle, Dad. Please?"

Isla decided to show Dad what a wonderful pet Pickle could be.

He could help them cut the grass...

and play with baby Harris!

Dad wasn't so sure.

So Pickle tried even harder.

He came to visit Isla at school...

at the beach...

and even at bedtime!

In the end, Dad and Farmer Jess said yes, and Pickle came to live with Isla's family for good. That's how Isla and Pickle became best friends.

Now Isla helps
Pickle eat the
right food...

and Pickle helps Isla eat up her vegetables.

Isla keeps Pickle's mane looking good...

and Pickle keeps Isla fit and healthy.

Isla plays Pickle's favourite game, Splashy Paddles...

and Pickle plays Isla's favourite game, Knights and Unicorns.

Dad is also glad that
Pickle came to stay.

He's much more fun than a goldfish!